Diploma Day

By Sierra Harimann
Illustrated by The Artifact Group

SCHOLASTIC INC.

New York   Toronto   London   Auckland

Sydney   Mexico City   New Delhi   Hong Kong

ISBN 978-0-545-28143-0

Published by Scholastic Inc. SCHOLASTIC and associated logos are trademarks and/or registered trademarks of Scholastic Inc.
Lexile is a registered trademark of MetaMetrics, Inc.

12 11 10 9 8 7 6 5 4 3 2 1   11 12 13 14 15 16/0

Designed by Angela Jun
Printed in the U.S.A.
First printing, May 2011   40

It was the last week of school at the Fashion Academy. The puppies were all looking forward to getting their diplomas.

"Hooray! It's almost Diploma Day!" Montana barked happily. "I can't wait for our end-of-the-year fashion show. I'm going to model my cute pink sweater. I designed and knit it myself."

"This fashion show is going to be marvelous, darlings," Gigi said in her French accent. She spun in a circle. "Don't you just love my polka-dotted tutu?"

3

"Yes, you look wonderful!" Ivy agreed. "And I can't wait to show off the sparkly collar I made."

Ivy turned to her friend Spike.

"What did you make for the fashion show?"

"I designed this red bandana," Spike told his friends. "I'm going to tie it around my neck, like this." Spike turned his head to show off his bandana.

Fuji pulled into the classroom on her scooter. Clarissa was close behind her. "What's up, puppies?" Fuji asked her friends.

"We're showing off our designs for the end-of-the-year fashion show," Montana said.

"Great idea!" Fuji barked happily. "Check out my beret!"

"I love it!" Clarissa said sweetly. "And I dyed this T-shirt myself."

"*Ooh la la!* How *chic*!" Gigi said. "Chic means 'stylish' in French."

Sammy and Elana were the last puppies to arrive.

"What are you both going to wear for the fashion show?" Clarissa asked them.

"I made this flowery clip out of fabric scraps and lace," Sammy said shyly. She turned her head so they could see it. "Do you like it?"

"It's beautiful!" Clarissa replied. "What about you, Elana?"

But Elana had her nose buried in her backpack. She seemed to be looking for something.

"Oh, no!" Elana gasped. "I can't find the shawl I sewed for the fashion show."

"Don't worry, Elana," Sammy said kindly. "We'll find your shawl."

"Yeah!" Clarissa agreed. "First, tell us what it looks like."

Elana thought about the shawl she had worked so hard on. "Well, it's dark purple with sparkly fringe."

"I remember seeing your shawl!" said Fuji. "You showed it to me at lunch the other day."

"You're right!" Elana barked. "The cafeteria was cold, so I put it on to warm up and to show you how it looked."

"Let's check the cafeteria first," Fuji suggested. "Maybe you left it there after lunch."

"Great idea," Montana agreed. "Don't worry, Elana. We'll find it!"

Elana nodded. She was so glad she had such wonderful friends.

"Come on, everyone," Ivy barked. "Let's make it work, puppies!"

The puppies sniffed the cafeteria from top to bottom.

"I haven't found anything," Sammy said.

Spike came out of the kitchen. "Sorry, Elana," he said. "I didn't find your shawl. But I did find a plate of peanut butter cookies."

"Yum!" Fuji said. "I think we could all use a snack break."

"Do you remember the day when we all got A's on our fashion quiz?" Spike asked as he munched on a cookie. "We got cookies during class as a special treat."

"That's right!" Ivy replied. "We all studied for that quiz together. And now we're graduating!"

"Speaking of graduating," Spike replied. "Why don't we try the auditorium? Maybe Elana left her shawl there after our graduation rehearsal this morning."

The puppies headed to the auditorium. Fritz the
stagehand was sweeping the stage.
"Hi, guys," Fritz said. "What's up?"

"We're looking for Elana's purple shawl," Sammy
barked. "Have you seen it anywhere?"

"Hmm, can't say I have," Fritz replied. "Sorry, Elana.
You might want to double-check backstage, though."

Sammy looked around backstage.

"Well, I didn't find your shawl, Elana," Sammy said. "But I did find the rack of costumes we designed together for *Rover and Juliet*."

"Working on the play together was the best," Fritz said happily.

"Ah, *oui!*" Gigi sighed wistfully. "Why don't we try on the costumes one more time, just for fun?"

"That's it!" Fuji cried. "I just remembered that Elana tried on her shawl last night at Puppyville Manor. I'm sure that's where it is!"

"You're right!" Elana exclaimed. "I must have left it in the living room at Puppyville Manor."

She turned to Fuji. "Thanks for remembering. I'm lucky to have such great friends."

The puppies headed straight to Puppyville Manor.
Elana was the first one in the door.
"Found it!" she called.
"Hooray!" the puppies cheered.

"We'd better get ready for the fashion show and graduation ceremony," Clarissa reminded everyone.

"Clarissa's right," Ivy barked. "The show starts in a few hours!"

A few hours later, it was time for the show.
The friends made their way down the puppywalk,
showing off each of their designs as the crowd clapped
and cheered.

When the fashion show was over, the puppies put on their graduation caps.

"Time to get our diplomas!" Ivy barked happily.
"We did it, puppies," Montana agreed. "Way to go!"

"Happy Diploma Day, everyone!" Elana barked.